Book 5

Ick and Crud

First Day of School

by Wiley Blevins • illustrated by Jim Paillot

RED CHAIR •PRESS•

Funny Bone Books

and Funny Bone Readers are produced and published by
Red Chair Press LLC   PO Box 333   South Egremont, MA 01258-0333
www.redchairpress.com

About the Author

Wiley Blevins has taught elementary school in both the United States and South America. He has also written over 60 books for children and 15 for teachers, as well as created reading programs for schools in the U.S. and Asia with Scholastic, Macmillan/McGraw-Hill, Houghton-Mifflin Harcourt, and other publishers. Wiley currently lives and writes in New York City.

About the Artist

Jim Paillot is a dad, husband and illustrator. He lives in Arizona with his family and two dogs and any other animal that wants to come in out of the hot sun. When not illustrating, Jim likes to hike, watch cartoons and collect robots.

Publisher's Cataloging-In-Publication Data

Names: Blevins, Wiley. | Paillot, Jim, illustrator.
Title: Ick and Crud. Book 5, First day of school / by Wiley Blevins; illustrated by Jim Paillot.
Other Titles: First day of school | Funny bone books. First chapters.

Description: South Egremont, MA: Red Chair Press, [2019] |
Summary: "Ick and Crud are off to school and they aren't sure what to expect."

Identifiers: ISBN 9781634402613 (hardcover) | ISBN 9781634402651 (paperback) |
ISBN 9781634402699 (ebook)

Subjects: LCSH: Friendship--Juvenile fiction. | First day of school--Juvenile fiction. | Dogs--Juvenile
fiction. | CYAC: Friendship--Fiction. | First day of school--Fiction. | Dogs--Fiction.

Classification: LCC PZ7.B618652 Icf 2019 (print) | LCC PZ7.B618652 (ebook)
| DDC [E]--dc23   LCCN: 2017957083

Printed in the United States of America
1018 1P CGBS19

Table of Contents

Meet the Characters

Crud

Ick

Miss Puffy

Bob

Mrs. Martin

A Brilliant Idea

"Where's Bob going?" asked Ick.

"He's grabbing our leashes," said Crud. "And you know what that means."

"Yes," said Ick. "It's time to take Bob for a walk."

"Where will we go this time?" asked Crud.

"Bob likes the lake," said Ick.

"Not after you pushed him in," said Crud.

"He looked hot," said Ick. "Well, what about the park?"

"We can't go there. Remember the squirrel attack? Putting nuts on Bob's hat was a bad idea."

"Bob's not easy to walk," said Ick.

"No, he isn't," said Crud. "But we must. He needs the exercise."

Ick and Crud yapped at Bob.

Bob snapped on their leashes.

"Hurry, Bob," they barked. Ick and Crud led him onto the sidewalk.

Crud lapped up the fresh air.

Ick hopped. He rolled in the leaves. He sneezed and barked at a butterfly. Then he suddenly stopped and looked up. Mrs. Martin was peeking over the fence.

"Where is you-know-who?" asked Ick.

"Don't ask," said Crud.

Miss Puffy hopped onto the fence. She licked her paws like they were lollipops.

"Hello, boys," she purred. "Out for a stroll?"

"Do you think she sees us?" asked Ick.

"I don't think so," said Crud. "Just keep moving." He tugged his leash to the right.

Ick tugged to the left. "Come on, Bob!"

"Oh, look," said Mrs. Martin. "Those two sure have a hard time on a leash. You know what they need?"

"What?" asked Bob.

"They need to go to school."

Bob nodded. "That's a brilliant idea!"

Miss Puffy hissed a laugh.

"School?" said Ick. "I'm not going to school."

"Me neither," said Crud. "In school they make you sit."

"And roll over."

"And play dead."

"Yeah," said Ick. "And play dead." He shivered thinking about it. "No way. No how. Not going to go." And as far as he was concerned, that was that.

Strike One

The next morning Bob set out two small crates. He tossed a bone into each crate.

"Uh-oh!" warned Crud. "Don't fall for that again." But before he finished, Ick was already inside. Gnawing on the bone.

Crud rolled his eyes. "Fine," he said. "To doggie school we go. But there better not be homework!" And in he waddled.

A big sign hung outside the school.
Bob carried Ick and Crud inside.

A teacher greeted them. His face was round and flat. His nose barely there.

"He looks like a bulldog," said Ick.

"Don't insult our bulldog friends," whispered Crud.

The teacher pointed to a line on the floor. It ran from one end of the room to the other.

"What are we doing?" asked Ick.

"The teacher is making us sit on this line," said Crud.

"Does it hurt?" asked Ick.

"It's not electric," said Crud. "Just sit."

Ick stood in front of the line and sniffed. He stood behind the line and sniffed. Then he stood over the line and wiggled his butt. Plop!

"Ah, that's better," he said. "But where is Bob going?"

Bob and the other humans walked to the opposite side of the room. The teacher stood beside them. As soon as he raised his hand, the room filled with dog names.

"Fifi and Fido. Santa Paws. Sir Barks-a-lot. Come! Come! Come!" shouted the humans.

Bob yelled, "Come Crud. Come Ick."

Ick sat and tilted his head. Crud licked his paw. "We're so much smarter than the other dogs," said Crud. "Look at how they run. They'll never train their humans that way."

Bob jumped up and down. He flapped his arms. "Come Crud. Come Ick," he screamed.

"This is fun," said Ick. "Look at Bob go. Is he trying to fly?"

"I think he's trying to dance," said Crud. "Should we go to him?"

"I will if you will," said Ick.

"Just wait," said Crud. "Let's see what else we can get Bob to do."

Bob jumped higher. He yelled louder. He waved his arms faster and faster. His face turned a sunny red. All the dogs sat quietly by their humans and watched. All but Ick and Crud. They stayed on the line. Crud rolled on his back and let out a moan. Ick licked the floor.

The teacher pointed at Ick and Crud. "Strike one," he said.

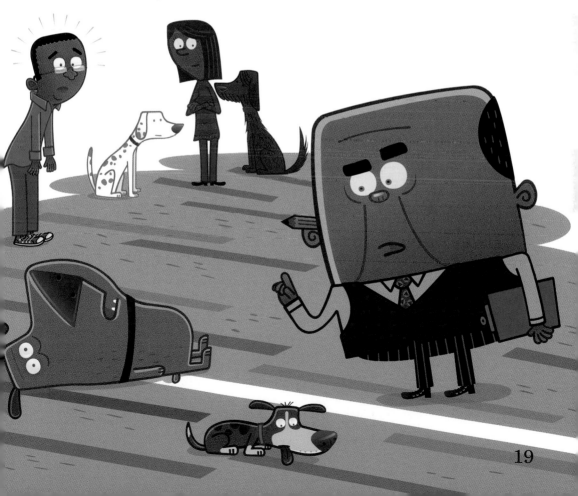

Strike Two

"What's next?" asked Ick. "This is fun."

"Maybe magic tricks," said Crud. "Look."

One at a time, each human lowered his or her hand and said "stay." Then the human started yelling a string of words. "Shoe. Sun. Pencil. Book." The human's dog stayed on the line.

"Good boy," said the teacher to the dog. "A well-trained dog only comes when he hears his name."

Then it was Bob's turn. He slowly lowered his hand. He looked into Ick's and Crud's eyes. "Stay," he said.

"Good boy, Bob," said Ick. "He learns fast."

"Just wait," said Crud.

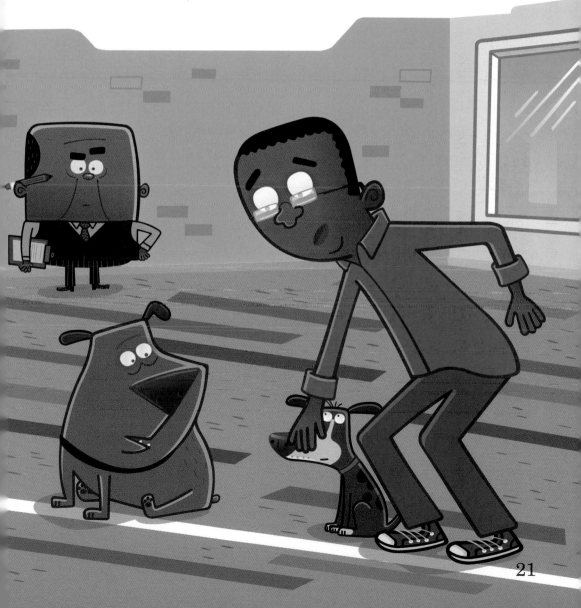

Bob took a deep breath. Then he yelled, "Shoe. Stick. Pickle!"

"Pickle?" asked Ick. "Does Bob have a pickle?

"Yum," said Crud. And the two raced across the room, jumping into Bob's arms.

The teacher frowned. "Strike two," he said.

teacher's PET

Strike Three

"That was fun," said Ick. "But next time there better be a pickle!"

Bob picked up Ick. He took him to the teacher. The teacher unwrapped a small purple sheet.

"This shows how smart your dog is," he said. "It takes most dogs only two or three seconds to get out from under it."

Bob gently placed the sheet over Ick.

"Oh, how warm," said Ick. He wiggled under the sheet. Then he sniffed the floor. "I smell you Crud," he barked. "Here I come." He waddled over to him. Crud crawled under the sheet to join Ick. Within seconds both were curled up and snoring.

"Strike three," moaned the teacher.

Bob plopped on the floor beside Ick and Crud. "Seriously, guys," he said. "What was that?" Ick peeked out from under the sheet. He leaned his head onto Bob's leg.

"Poor Bob," said Ick.

"He's not so good at school," said Crud.

The Big Test

"Okay, class," said the teacher. "Here's the big test for today. Put your dogs on the line." The humans did as they were told. They looked nervous. All the dogs sat. A few wiggled and wagged.

Ick rolled his eyes. "They do whatever their human says."

"Yeah," said Crud. "Will they ever learn? It's the humans that need to be trained. And it takes time!"

"Now," whispered the teacher. "Make your dog stay seated for one minute. Any dog who can sit that long passes the test."

"I like to sit," said Crud.

"I can sit all day," said Ick. And he started licking the air.

The humans kneeled low to the floor. Chants of "stay, stay, stay" filled the room. Bob looked at Ick and Crud. Sweat dripped down his face. "Stay," he pleaded. "Please, please stay."

"You don't have to ask me twice," said Ick. He rolled over and stared at the ceiling. Crud rolled beside him.

Just then Mrs. Martin walked outside the class window. On her shoulder sat Miss Puffy. She swished her tail from side to side. And she hissed at Ick and Crud.

All the dogs shot across the room. They banged against the window. Growling and barking. Miss Puffy arched her back and hissed some more.

Ick and Crud didn't move. Not a foot. Not an inch. Not even an eensy-weensy centimeter. "If they only knew her," said Ick.

"Yeah, they would have stayed with us," said Crud.

The teacher handed Bob a certificate. It had a big gold star on it. "I don't know how," he said. "But Ick and Crud passed the test. Good luck with them!" He shook his head and walked away.

"Are you ready to go home?" asked Crud.

"I am," said Ick. "All this schooling is giving me a headache. Bob's not easy to train."

"I wonder what we can teach him next?" asked Crud.

"Hold the doggie door," said Ick. "Maybe we can teach Bob to fetch. Balls. Sticks. And lots of food."

"Good idea, buddy," said Crud. "Let's go home and get started."